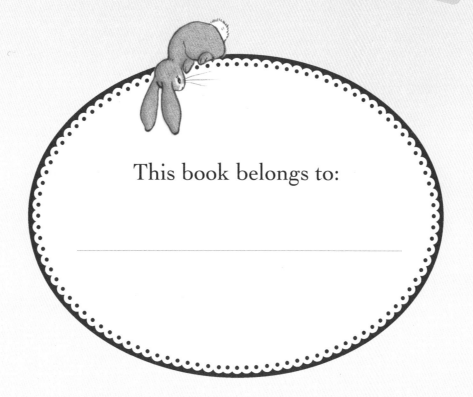

This book belongs to:

_____

To Kate and Patrick for trusting me . . .
. . . and Mark for understanding my passion.

ORCHARD BOOKS
Carmelite House
50 Victoria Embankment
London EC4Y 0DZ

First published in 2015 by Orchard Books

ISBN 978 1 40833 708 0

Text © Mark Sperring 2015
Illustrations © Mandy Sutcliffe 2015

The rights of Mark Sperring to be identified as the author and Mandy Sutcliffe to be identified
as the illustrator of this work have been asserted by them in accordance with the
Copyright, Designs and Patents Act, 1988.

A CIP catalogue record for this book is available from the British Library.

1 3 5 7 9 10 8 6 4 2

Printed in China

Orchard Books
An imprint of Hachette Children's Group
Part of The Watts Publishing Group Limited
An Hachette UK Company
www.hachette.co.uk

Hop Along Boo

Time For Bed

Mandy Sutcliffe

With words by Mark Sperring

ORCHARD

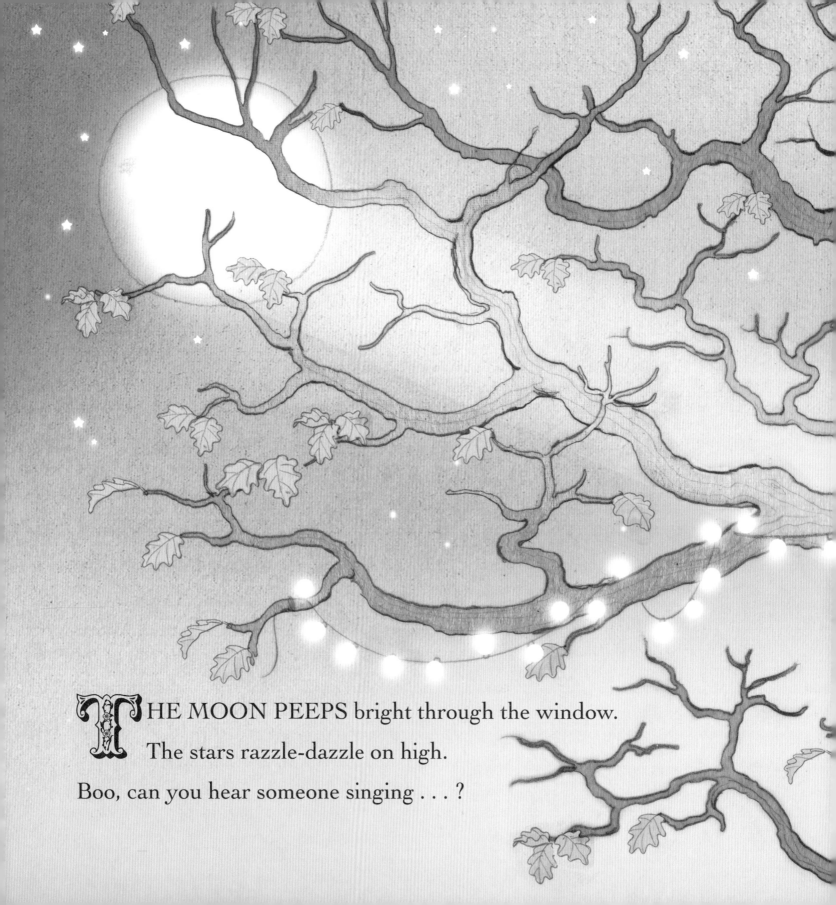

THE MOON PEEPS bright through the window.

The stars razzle-dazzle on high.

Boo, can you hear someone singing . . . ?

Belle's singing a lullaby!

She's strumming a sleepy old song now,
Singing, "Boo, it's time for your bed!"
So, Boo, don't you bunny around now.
The pillow's awaiting your head!

The whole world is snug in their jim-jams.
They've all brushed their teeth till they gleam.
They're all skipping out of the bathroom,
And heading off into a dream.

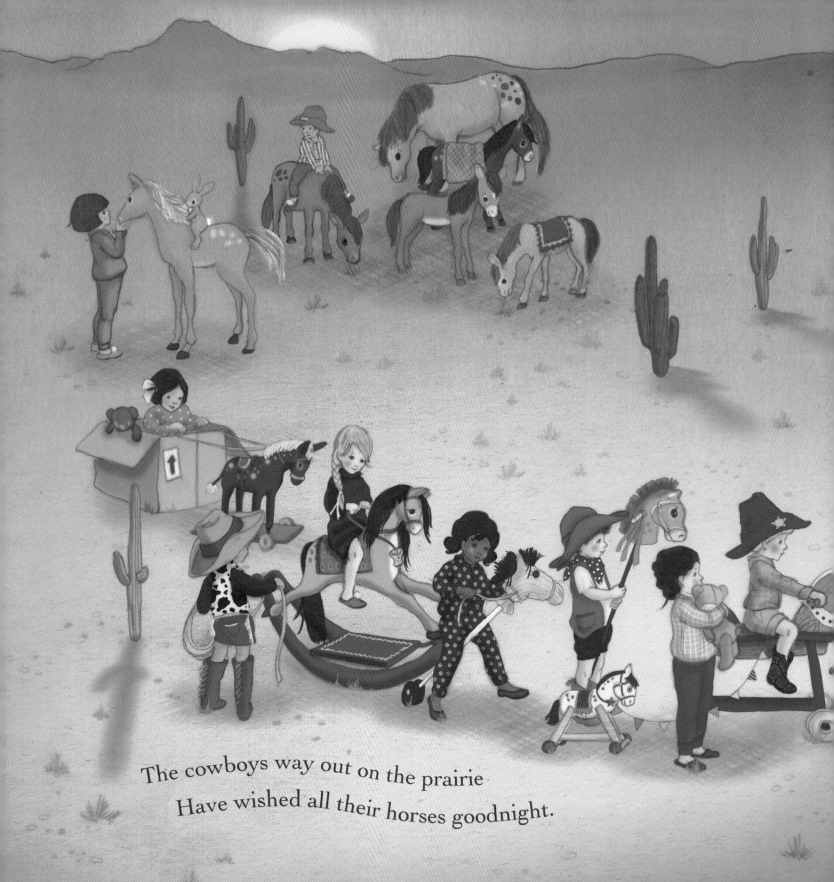

The cowboys way out on the prairie
Have wished all their horses goodnight.

They're climbing the stairs up to bed now,
While holding their teddy bears tight!

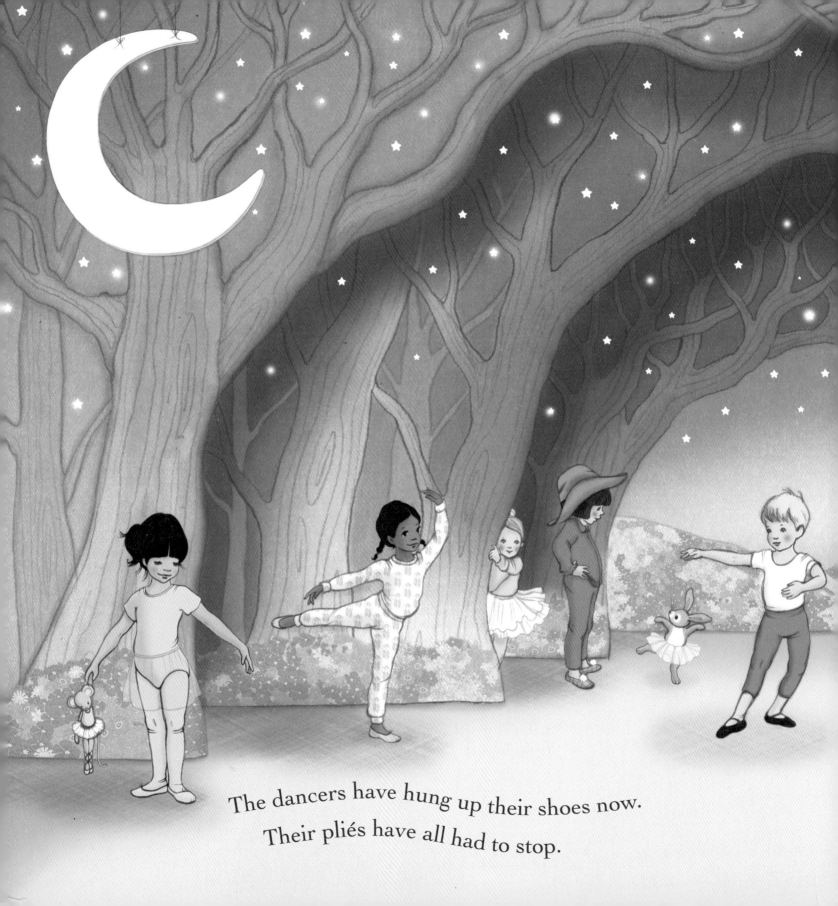

The dancers have hung up their shoes now.
Their pliés have all had to stop.

So, Boo, point your toes towards bed now,
And spring up those stairs with a hop!

The fairies, they flew up so sprightly,
Their wings glittered in the moon's glow . . .

. . . But the elephants thumped up like thunder.

I don't think they wanted to go!

All the babies are snug in their cots now,
As comfy as babies can be.
The toddlers have all toddled off now –
Just time for a story . . . or three!

All the big ships have dropped anchor – sploosh!
Little sailors are resting their heads.
Pirates are snoozing in hammocks.
Captain Boo, it's time for your bed!

So, Boo, there's no time for games now.
For most of the world's fast asleep.
And Belle's little song has turned into a . . .

... YAAAAAAAAAAAWN!

So hop to it, Boo.

Move those feet!

Bedtime and blankets are waiting.
Cuddles and snuggles are too.

On a pillow as soft as a feather,

Let's whisper . . .

. . . "Goodnight, Belle and Boo."